OKOMI
Plays in the Leaves

Helen and
Clive Dorman

Illustrated by
Tony Hutchings

Dawn Publications
in association with The Jane Goodall Institute

One day, Okomi and his mommy, Mama Du, were going for a walk. Okomi liked going for walks with his mommy.

He liked to run ahead and explore.

It was a lovely day and there
was a gentle breeze.

A leaf fluttered down from one
of the trees.
It landed on Okomi's nose!

Okomi was so surprised
that he jumped, spun around,
and plopped to the ground
with a bump!

Suddenly there were other
leaves falling from above.
In fact, there were leaves
falling all around.

Okomi thought it was
very exciting.

He jumped up and down,
trying to catch
the falling leaves.
He spun round and round.
He even did a somersault!

Okomi was having
a wonderful time.

He scooped the leaves
into a big pile.

The pile grew bigger and bigger
until Okomi could not
see over the top.

Then he jumped into the pile
and rolled over and over
in them.

He threw handfuls of leaves
up in the air above his head.
They landed all over
his face and nose.

Oops! A handful of leaves
fluttered over his shoulder
and landed right on
Mama Du's face!

Mama Du brushed the leaves
from her face and laughed.

Okomi jumped into the pile of leaves again and rolled over. This time they covered him completely.

Mama Du couldn't see
Okomi anywhere.
She looked and looked but still
she couldn't see him.

Can you see Okomi?

Suddenly, the big pile of leaves
began to move.

"Ooo, Ooo, Ooo" laughed Okomi
as he jumped out of the leaves.

Mama Du was very surprised!
She was also very pleased to
see her little Okomi again.

The Work Of Jane Goodall

For many years, Jane Goodall patiently watched chimpanzees in the African forest. She saw chimp babies play with their mothers and that chimpanzees have close family ties. She saw young chimps throw tantrums and have exciting learning adventures. She saw that the chimpanzee mother-infant relationship is virtually identical to its human counterpart.

Jane Goodall's research of more than 40 years showed how chimpanzees reason and solve problems, how they make tools and use them, and how they communicate. It revealed that they have a wide range of emotions. It showed that each of them has a unique, vivid personality. Indeed, their genetic makeup is closer to us than any other animal—with almost 99% identical DNA. Jane's revolutionary work bids us to look upon chimpanzees as non-human relatives.

Jane with an orphan chimpanzee

Photo by Michael Neugebauer

Yet the plight of these "relatives" is desperate. Their forests are being cut down. They are being hunted for food. Their numbers are dwindling drastically. And when chimpanzee mothers are killed, the orphaned babies—often taken to be sold illegally as pets—cannot be returned successfully to the wild.

When Jane realized that chimpanzees were becoming endangered, she began a worldwide effort on their behalf. She campaigns tirelessly, and established The Jane Goodall Institute. It has created sanctuaries for orphan chimpanzees. (You can help the orphans by "adopting a chimp.") It works to improve conditions in zoos and laboratories, and to halt deforestation and the bushmeat trade. The Institute also

Fanni and her baby, Fax.

sponsors Roots & Shoots, a worldwide program for young people working to make a difference for animals, the environment and their communities. For more information contact The Jane Goodall Institute, P.O. Box 14890, Silver Spring, MD 20910, or call (301) 565-0086, or go to www.janegoodall.org.

DAWN PUBLICATIONS
A SHARING NATURE WITH CHILDREN BOOK

Part of the proceeds from the sale of this book supports the work of The Jane Goodall Institute's Tchimpounga Sanctuary in the Congo Republic. Dawn Publications is dedicated to inspiring in children a deeper understanding and appreciation for all life on Earth. To view our full list of titles, or to order, please visit our web site at www.dawnpub.com, or call 800-545-7475.

A Sharing Nature With Children Book

Published by arrangement with The Children's Project Ltd., P.O. Box 2, Richmond, TW10 7FL, U.K., and the Jane Goodall Institute Ltd., 15 Clarendon Park, Lymington, Hants SO41 8AX, U.K.

Library of Congress Cataloging-in-Publication Data

Dorman, Helen.
  Okomi : plays in the leaves / Helen and Clive Dorman ; illustrated by Tony Hutchings. -- 1st ed.
       p. cm. -- (A sharing nature with children book)
Summary: On a walk with his Mama Du, Okomi is fascinated by falling leaves and has fun playing with them.
  ISBN 1-58469-047-X (pbk.)
  1. Chimpanzees -- Juvenile fiction. [1. Chimpanzees--Fiction. 2. Animals -- Infancy -- Fiction.] I. Dorman, Clive. II. Hutchings, Tony, ill. III. Title. IV Series.
  PZ10.3.D7185 Ome 2003
  [E] -- dc21
                2002015161

Dawn Publications
P.O. Box 2010
Nevada City, CA 95959
530-478-0111
nature@dawnpub.com
www.dawnpub.com

Printed in Korea

10 9 8 7 6 5 4 3 2 1
First Edition
Design and computer production by Andrea Miles